The Primary Source Library of the Thirteen Colonies and The Lost Colony™

The Colony of New York

A Primary Source History

The Rosen Publishing Group's
PowerKids Press™
PRIMARY SOURCE

Melody S. Mis

To Judith and Gary Thomas, who count New York as their favorite destination

Published in 2007 by The Rosen Publishing Group, Inc.
29 East 21st Street, New York, NY 10010

First Edition

Editor: Jennifer Way
Book Design: Ginny Chu
Layout Design: Julio A. Gil
Photo Researcher: Amy Feinberg

Photo Credits: Cover, pp. 8 (inset), 18 (inset) © New-York Historical Society, New York, USA/Bridgeman Art Library; p. 4 © New York Public Library /Science Source /Getty Images; pp. 4, 8 I.N. Phelps Stokes Collection, Miriam and Ira D. Wallach Division of Art, Prints and Photographs, The New York Public Library, Astor, Lenox and Tilden Foundations; p. 4 (inset) © The British Library/HIP/The Image Works; p. 6 © 1986 L.F. Tantillo, (inset) The New Netherland Institute; p. 10 © Bettmann/Contributor/ Bettmann/Getty Images; p. 10 (inset) © Bridgeman Art Library/Getty Images; p. 10 © Museum of the City of New York/Corbis; p. 12 Courtesy of the New York State Archives; p. 12 (inset) Private Collection, © Christie's Images/Bridgeman Art Library; pp. 14, 20 Library of Congress, Geography and Map Division; p. 14 (inset) Library of Congress, Rare Book and Special Collections Division, Printed Ephemera Collection; p. 16 © Mary Evans Picture Library/The Image Works; p. 16 (inset) Collection of The New-York Historical Society; p. 18 Emmet Collection, Miriam and Ira D. Wallach Division of Art, Prints and Photographs, The New York Public Library, Astor, Lenox and Tilden Foundations; p. 20 (inset) Chateau de Versailles, France, Giraudon/ Bridgeman Art Library.

Library of Congress Cataloging-in-Publication Data

Mis, Melody S.
    The colony of New York : a primary source history / Melody S. Mis.
        p. cm. — (The primary source library of the thirteen colonies and the Lost Colony)
    Includes index.
    ISBN 1-4042-3432-2 (library binding) — ISBN 1-4042-2135-2 (pbk.)
    1. New York (State)—History—Colonial period, ca. 1600–1775—Juvenile literature. 2. New York (State)—History—1775–1865—Juvenile literature. 3. New York (State)—History—Colonial period, ca. 1600–1775—Sources—Juvenile literature. 4. New York (State)—History—1775–1865—Sources—Juvenile literature. I. Title. II. Series.
    F122.M67 2007
    974.7'02—dc22

                                    2005026681

Contents

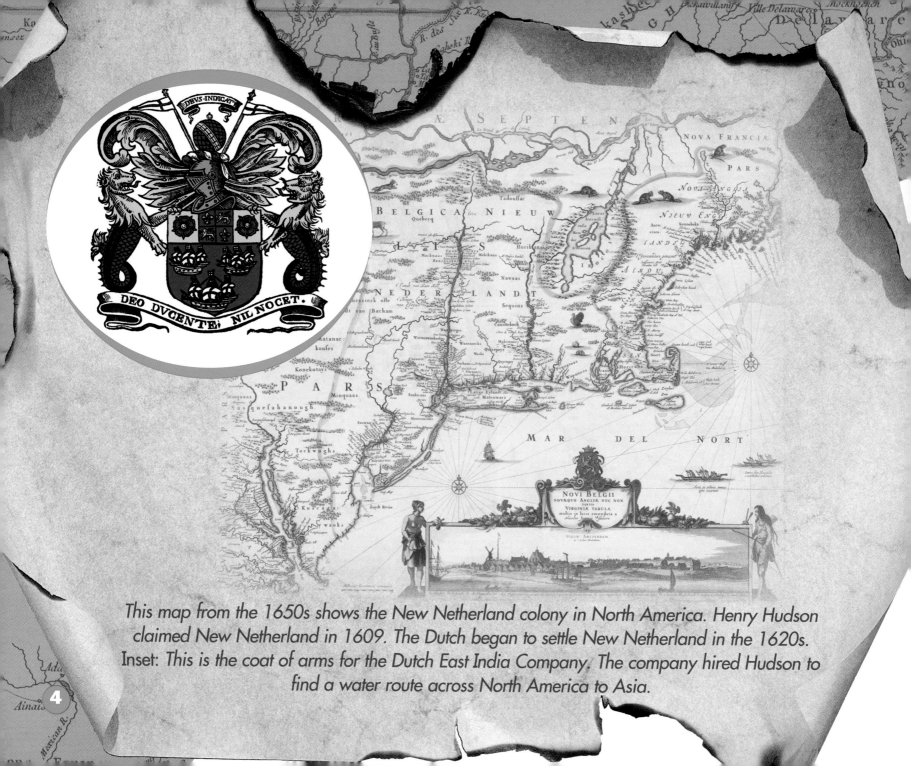

This map from the 1650s shows the New Netherland colony in North America. Henry Hudson claimed New Netherland in 1609. The Dutch began to settle New Netherland in the 1620s. Inset: This is the coat of arms for the Dutch East India Company. The company hired Hudson to find a water route across North America to Asia.

Discovering New York

Before Europeans came to New York, it had been settled for many years by Native Americans. These Native Americans were living in New York when the first Europeans landed in North America.

The Italian Giovanni da Verrazano was the first European to explore New York. He sailed into New York Harbor in 1524, looking for a water **route** through North America to Asia. At that time ships traveled around South America to reach Asia. When Verrazano did not find a new route, he returned to Europe.

In 1609, the Englishman Henry Hudson arrived in New York and sailed up the river that was later named for him. Hudson had been hired by the Netherlands' Dutch East India Company to find a water route to Asia. Although he did not find it, he claimed New York for the Netherlands and named it New Netherland.

From West India Company Letter

"High and Mighty Lords, Yesterday the ship the Arms of Amsterdam arrived here. It sailed from New Netherland out of the River Mauritius on the 23rd of September. They report that our people are in good spirit and live in peace. . . . They have purchased the Island Manhattes from the Indians for the value of 60 guilders."

Peter Schaghen of the West India Company wrote this letter to report to the company about the New Netherland colony. This letter also says that New Amsterdam's governor, Peter Minuit, had purchased Manhattan Island from Native Americans. This land would become part of New York City.

The Dutch West India Company established Fort Orange in 1624. This painting shows what the settlement would have looked like in 1635. The fort was surrounded by water, which helped keep the fort safe. Inset: This is a letter written to the Dutch West India Company in 1626.

Early Dutch Settlers

In the 1600s, Dutch ships traveled to New Netherland to trade with the Iroquois Native Americans. Merchants in the Netherlands wanted to make money from trading North American furs. The merchants formed the Dutch West India Company in 1621, to set up trading posts in North America.

In 1624, the Dutch West India Company sent about 110 people from the Netherlands to establish the Fort Orange colony in what is now Albany, New York. Many of the colonists were French-speaking **Protestants**. The Dutch West India Company got the Protestants to go to New York by telling them they could practice their religion freely there.

Five different groups made up the Iroquois. These were the Mohawk, the Seneca, the Onondaga, the Oneida, and the Cayuga. They often fought each other. In the 1500s, they decided to quit fighting and form one nation. Each group governed itself and chose people to serve in the Iroquois government. The government was created to work out the nation's problems peacefully.

This 1660 map shows New Amsterdam. The line on the right is the log wall that settlers put up to guard the city. The place where the log fence was located is today's Wall Street. Inset: Peter Stuyvesant's improvements to New Amsterdam led more people to move there. He was governor of New Amsterdam from 1647 until 1664.

Settling New Amsterdam

In 1626, the Dutch West India Company established a colony in New York on the island of Manhattan. The colony was called New Amsterdam, after a city in the Netherlands. The colonists built a log fence at one end of the settlement to keep it safe.

During the late 1620s, New Amsterdam grew quickly. Its harbors on the Atlantic Ocean and the Hudson River drew trading ships from all over the world. In 1626, Dutch ships brought the first African slaves to New Amsterdam.

In 1647, Peter Stuyvesant became the governor of New Amsterdam. He was a **strict** leader, but he worked to improve the city.

Wampum was the name that Native Americans gave the beads that they made. The Native Americans used wampum to tell stories. They did this by creating interesting shapes with the beads on belts. A special tribe member, called the keeper of the wampum, remembered the story that went with each shape. After the colonists arrived in New York, wampum was used as a form of money.

Smugglers who brought goods to the English colonies through New Amsterdam's harbor, shown here, avoided paying England's shipping taxes. These taxes controlled the colonies' shipping practices and were called the Navigation Acts. Inset: Charles II was king of England from 1660 until 1685.

The English Claim New Netherland

New Netherland was located between the English colonies in New England and the English colonies in the South. New Netherland became a problem for England. **Smugglers** were using the port of New Amsterdam to avoid having to pay England's shipping taxes. Merchants smuggled goods to and from the colonies through New Netherland. This angered the English king, Charles II.

In 1664, Charles II decided that the only way England could control the colonies' shipping practices was to make New Netherland an English colony. He told his brother, James, that he could have control of the colony. James, who was the Duke of York, sent warships to New Amsterdam. The colonists in New Amsterdam did not put up a fight and lost the city to the English. After the English claimed New Amsterdam, they renamed the colony New York.

In 1664, James, Duke of York, was granted a proprietary charter for land that included New York. The charter gave James the power to force the Dutch to give New Amsterdam to the English. The charter also put James in control of the colony. Inset: When James became King James II, New York became a royal colony.

New York Becomes a Royal Colony

Under James, New York became a **proprietary colony**. Most proprietary **charters** allowed colonies to have an **elected assembly**. James's charter did not. This meant that New Yorkers did not have a voice in their government.

In the beginning James tried to be fair to the colonists. He allowed the Dutch colonists to keep their land. He also continued to allow religious freedom. When James became King James II of England in 1685, New York's proprietary charter became a royal charter. That meant that the king controlled the colony. In 1689, New Yorkers **rebelled** against the Colonial government. Jacob Leisler became the colonists' leader for almost two years. In 1691, the English ordered Leisler to step down. Leisler refused, and he was hanged by the English. This period is sometimes called Leisler's Rebellion.

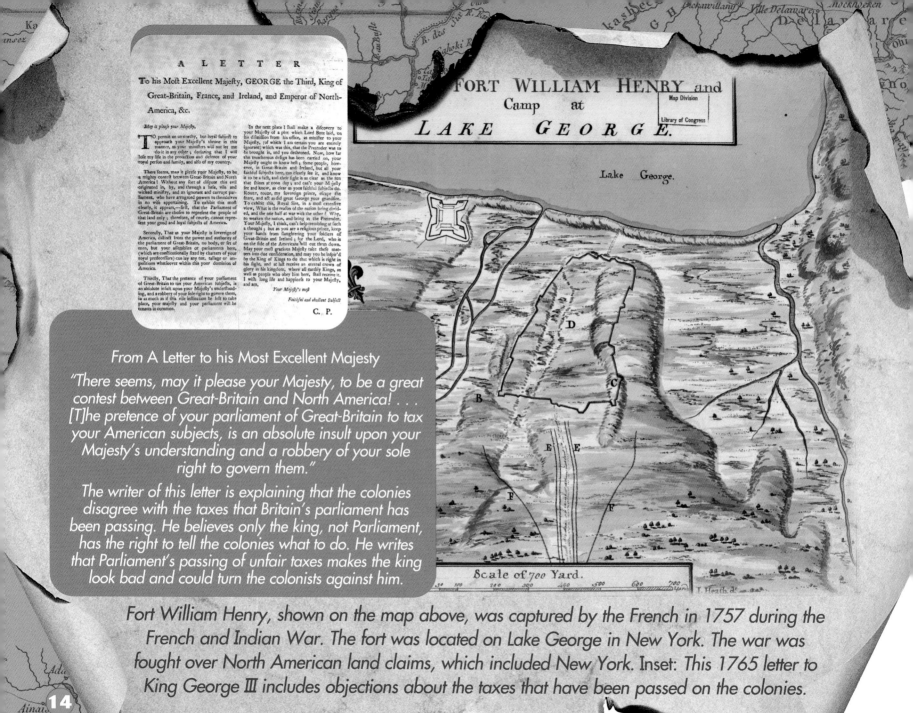

A LETTER

To his Most Excellent Majesty, GEORGE the Third, King of Great-Britain, France, and Ireland, and Emperor of North-America, &c.

From A Letter to his Most Excellent Majesty

"There seems, may it please your Majesty, to be a great contest between Great-Britain and North America! . . . [T]he pretence of your parliament of Great-Britain to tax your American subjects, is an absolute insult upon your Majesty's understanding and a robbery of your sole right to govern them."

The writer of this letter is explaining that the colonies disagree with the taxes that Britain's parliament has been passing. He believes only the king, not Parliament, has the right to tell the colonies what to do. He writes that Parliament's passing of unfair taxes makes the king look bad and could turn the colonists against him.

Fort William Henry, shown on the map above, was captured by the French in 1757 during the French and Indian War. The fort was located on Lake George in New York. The war was fought over North American land claims, which included New York. Inset: This 1765 letter to King George III includes objections about the taxes that have been passed on the colonies.

Britain Taxes the Colonies

From the time of James II's rule through the 1700s, Britain began to pass laws and taxes without the approval of the colonies' elected assemblies. This was against the colonies' charters. The colonies believed Britain only cared about the money that it got from the colonists, and that made them angry.

The colonists became even angrier after the **French and Indian War**, which was fought between 1754 and 1763. Since the war was fought on American soil, Britain wanted the colonies to pay for the war. To raise money Britain taxed the colonies on many goods, such as tea, sugar, and cloth, that were shipped to the colonies.

These laws and taxes hurt the colonies. Most colonists could not afford to buy sugar, coffee, and other taxed items. In reply to these taxes, the colonies began to protest, or act out, against Britain.

Joy to AMERICA!

New-York, May 20, 1766.

At 3 this Day arrived here an Express from *Boston* with the following most glorious News, on which *H. Gaine* congratulates the Friends of *America*.

Boston, Friday 11 o'Clock, 16th May, 1766.

This Day arrived here the Brig *Harrison*, belonging to *John Hancock*, Esq; Capt. *Shubael Coffin*, in 6 Weeks and 2 Days from *London*, with the following most agreeable Intelligence, viz.

From the *LONDON GAZETTE*.

Westminster, March 18.

THIS day his Majesty came to the house of Peers, and being in his royal robes, seated on the throne, with the usual solemnity, Sir *Francis Molineaux*, Gentleman usher of the black rod was sent with a Message from his Majesty to the house of commons, commanding their attendance in the house of peers. The commons being come thither accordingly, his Majesty was pleased to give his Royal Assent to

An ACT to Repeal an Act, made the last Session of Parliament, entitled, An Act for granting and applying certain stamp Duties, and other Duties in the *British* Colonies and Plantations in *America*, towards further defraying the Expences of defending, protecting, and securing the same; and for mending such Parts of the several Acts of Parliament relating to the Trade and Revenues of the said Colonies and Plantations, as direct the Manner of determining and recovering the Penalties and Forfeitures therein mentioned.

When his Majesty went to the House he was accompanied by greater Numbers of People than ever was known on the like Occasion; many Copies of the Repeal were sent to Falmouth, to be forwarded to America; and all the Vessels in the River Thames bound to America, had Orders to sail.

3 o'Clock, P. M. Since composing the Above an Express arrived from Philadelphia with a Confirmation of the Repeal, and that a printed Copy of it by the King's Printer lay in the Coffee-House for the Perusal of the Publick.

From Joy to America!

"At 3 this Day arrived here an Express from Boston with the following most glorious News. . . . [H]is Majesty was pleased to give his Royal Assent to An ACT to Repeal an Act, made the last Session of Parliament."

The article in this New York broadside was originally printed in Britain's London Gazette. It was then brought to Boston before it reached New York. It was common at the time for news to travel this way. The article says that the king agreed to end the Stamp Act at the last meeting of Parliament.

In this woodcut British troops are shown bringing the hated Stamp Act stamps to City Hall in New York City in 1765. Inset: This newspaper article is about the ending of the unpopular Stamp Act in 1766. Although the tax was ended on March 18, word did not reach New York until two months later.

16

New York Protests Taxation

The colonists were angry about the new taxes. The 1765 Stamp Act forced colonists to pay a tax on paper goods. **Representatives** from New York and other colonies met in New York City to protest. Some colonists boycotted, or refused to buy, British goods. The British ended the tax in 1766 because the boycotts caused many problems.

The Quartering Act was another law that made New Yorkers angry. It said that colonists had to house British soldiers who were stationed in their cities. New Yorkers refused to do this. In return for New York's refusal, Britain took away their elected assembly. Things became worse when Britain passed the Coercive Acts, which **punished** the colonies for their protests. New Yorkers began to feel they would not be able to work out their problems with Britain. They joined other colonists who were starting to push for independence.

The first reading of the Declaration of Independence in New York was on July 9, 1776. Inset: John Jay did not at first want the colonies to be independent from Britain. He hoped that the colonies could work out their problems with Britain. He later became a backer of independence.

New York Declares Independence

Some colonists, called patriots, wanted the colonies to become independent of Britain. On September 5, 1774, members from the 13 colonies met in Philadelphia, Pennsylvania, for the First Continental Congress to talk about breaking away from Britain. John Jay represented New York at the congress.

On April 19, 1775, a battle between British soldiers and a small group of patriots took place in Lexington, Massachusetts. It was the beginning of the **American Revolution**. One year later, on July 4, 1776, the Second Continental Congress approved the **Declaration of Independence**, which stated that the 13 colonies were free from British rule. At first John Jay did not sign the declaration. He later changed his mind, signed the declaration, and backed the war. After New York approved the declaration, the state set up its own government.

PLAN OF THE POSITION which the ARMY under Lt Genl BURGOYNE took at S.
on the 10th of September 1777, and in which it remained till THE CONVENTION was signed

HUDSONS RIVER

When the Continental army won the Battle of Saratoga in 1777, it was the first time other countries believed that the colonies could win the war. This helped sway countries, such as France, to help the colonists. Inset: Lafayette, a Frenchman, joined the Continental army as a major general in 1777. He also helped sway France to aid the colonies during the war.

The American Revolution in New York

In the summer of 1776, the Revolution spread to New York. The British sent warships to New York City. The British beat the Continental army and occupied the city for the rest of the war. While the British were there, fires broke out. Some people believed that the colonists were trying to burn British-occupied New York City to the ground.

The British were winning most of the battles during the first years of the war. The Americans needed help, but other countries did not believe that the colonists could win against rich and powerful Britain. In October 1777, the Americans finally won an important battle at Saratoga, New York. This made the French think that the Americans could beat the British. France then sent troops and supplies to the colonies. In October 1781, the war ended when General Washington's Continental army beat the British at Yorktown, Virginia.

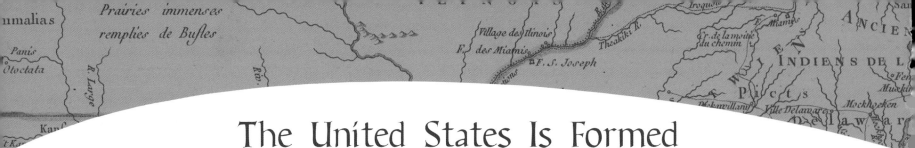

The United States Is Formed

The American Revolution officially ended in 1783, with the Treaty of Paris. New York City became the nation's **temporary** capital that year. In May 1787, representatives from the colonies met in Philadelphia, for the **Constitutional Convention**, to create a government.

Alexander Hamilton, Robert Yates, and John Lansing Jr. represented New York at the convention. The members of the convention talked about different ideas for the government. Hamilton was in favor of a national government that was stronger than those of the states. This is what the United States has today. When the **Constitution** was written, Hamilton signed it. Yates and Lansing did not, because they wanted stronger state governments. New York became the eleventh state after it approved the Constitution on July 26, 1788.

Glossary

American Revolution (uh-MER-uh-ken reh-vuh-LOO-shun) Battles that soldiers from the colonies fought against Britain for freedom, from 1775 to 1783.

charters (CHAR-turz) Official agreements giving someone permission to do something.

Constitution (kon-stuh-TOO-shun) The basic rules by which the United States is governed.

Constitutional Convention (kon-stuh-TOO-shuh-nul kun-VEN-shun) A meeting of members from the 13 colonies to create a body of laws for the newly formed United States of America.

Declaration of Independence (deh-kluh-RAY-shun UV in-duh-PEN-dints) An official announcement signed on July 4, 1776, in which American colonists stated they were free of British rule.

elected assembly (ih-LEK-ted uh-SEM-blee) A meeting with a lot of people who were chosen by their peers to attend.

French and Indian War (FRENCH AND IN-dee-un WOR) The battles fought between 1754 and 1763 by England, France, and Native Americans for control of North America.

proprietary colony (pruh-PRY-uh-ter-ee KAH-luh-nee) A privately owned colony or settlement.

Protestants (PRAH-tes-tunts) People who belong to a Christian-based church but who are not Catholic.

punished (PUN-ishd) Caused someone pain or loss for a crime he or she has committed.

rebelled (rih-BELD) Disobeyed the people or country in charge.

representatives (reh-prih-ZEN-tuh-tivz) People chosen to speak for others.

route (ROOT) The path a person takes to get somewhere.

smugglers (SMUH-glurz) People who sneak things in and out of a country.

strict (STRIKT) Very careful in following a rule or making others follow it.

temporary (TEM-puh-rer-ee) Lasting for a short amount of time.

Index

Primary Sources

Page 4. Map of North America. Hand-colored engraving, circa 1655, published by Nicolaes Visscher, The New York Public Library, New York, NY. **Page 6. Inset.** Letter to the West India Company. November 7, 1626, Peter Schaghen, The New Netherland Institute, Albany, NY. **Page 8.** Map of New Amsterdam. Drawing after land survey by Jacques Cortelyou, circa 1670, unknown artist, The New York Public Library, New York, NY. **Page 8. Inset.** *Governor Peter Stuyvesant.* Oil on panel, circa 1660, Hendrick Courturier, New-York Historical Society, New York, NY. **Page 10.** *New Amsterdam, Now New York, on the Island of Manhattan.* Painting, seventeenth century, Johannes Vinckeboons, Museum of the City of New York, New York, NY. **Page 10. Inset.** *Charles II.* Oil on canvas, circa seventeenth century, English School, Bridgeman Art Library, St. Edmunds College, Cambridge, UK. **Page 12.** Duke's charter. 1664, New York State Archives, Albany, NY. **Page 12. Inset.** *King James II.* Oil on canvas, circa seventeenth century, Sir Godfrey Kneller, Bridgeman Art Library, Private collection. **Page 14.** *Plan of Fort William Henry and Camp at Lake George.* Pen and ink and watercolor, circa 1755, Joseph Heath, Library of Congress, Washington, D.C. **Page 14. Inset.** *A letter to his Most Excellent Majesty.* 1765, Library of Congress, Washington, D.C. **Page 16. Inset.** *Joy to America!* May 20, 1776, New York Historical Society, New York, NY. **Page 18. Inset.** *John Jay.* Oil on canvas, circa eighteenth century, Joseph Wright of Derby, The New York Public Library, New York, NY. **Page 20.** *Plan of the position which the army under Lt. Genl. Burgoyne took at Saratoga.* Pen and ink, circa 1777, Library of Congress, Washington, D.C. **Page 20. Inset.** *General Lafayette.* Oil on canvas, 1791, Joseph Desire Court, Bridgeman Art Library, Chateau de Versailles, France.

Web Sites

Due to the changing nature of Internet links, PowerKids Press has developed an online list of Web sites related to the subject of this book. This site is updated regularly. Please use this link to access the list: www.powerkidslinks.com/pstclc/newyork/